1

A Bad Day to Be Sick

Akira blew her nose just as there was a knock on the apartment door.

"It's probably Diego," she said to her grandmother.

"Akira," her grandmother said. "I thought you were going to tell him you're sick."

Akira groaned. "I forgot."

Akira hated being sick. She especially hated being sick only three days before her birthday. But most of all, she hated being sick when she had things to do. Her favorite park had been sold. It was about to be destroyed. She needed to help Diego collect signatures to save it.

Diego and Akira loved hanging out at the park. It was right next to their apartment building. Sometimes, they played with Diego's little pug, Baya. Sometimes, they sat on their favorite bench talking about places they wanted to go to someday.

More than anything though, Akira loved the Wishing Tree that was in the park. Every year on Akira's birthday, her family tied wishes to it. If the park was sold, the Wishing Tree would be too. Her stomach knotted thinking about it.

Akira's grandmother walked to the door. "I'll tell Diego to come back tomorrow."

Akira sat up. "We can't wait until tomorrow!"

"Diego heard that there might be a meeting about the park soon. We need to prove that everyone loves the park," Akira explained.

Her grandmother opened the door to let Diego and Baya come inside. "I'd stay by the door unless you want to get sick too," she said to Diego.

"It's just a cold." Akira scowled. "Do you have the petition?"

Diego bent to remove his shoes. Then, he held up a clipboard. "Mr. Crock helped me type it up."

Mr. Crock lived in their building and taught tai chi in the park. A few days ago, Akira heard that he was buying the park. Since he always looked so grumpy, Akira and Diego were nervous to ask him about it. But they found out he loved the park too! He even suggested the petition.

Akira stood up. "Great! Let's go," she said to Diego.

Akira's grandma crossed her arms. "Do you want to get the whole building sick?"

Akira fell back onto the couch. "I guess we'll have to wait until tomorrow," she told Diego.

Diego looked down, in**spect**ing this clipboard. Talking to strangers norm**al**ly made him nervous. But if there really was a meeting soon, they needed to be ready. "I can do it," he said.

Akira wasn't sure that was a good idea. Diego wasn't great at talking to people. Plus, the Wishing Tree was more important to her than it was to Diego.

"You should wait for me," she said firmly. "I mean, you're afraid to talk to strangers. I'm not."

Diego frowned. "I'm trying," he said softly. He turned away but not before Akira saw the hurt in his eyes.

Guilt gripped Akira's stomach. She only meant that it would be easier if they did it together. But before she could explain, Diego and Baya had left.

2

Parts of the Whole

When Akira looked up, her grandmother was kneeling on the floor. The things she used in her tea ceremony were on the table between them.

"Would you like tea?" she asked. Akira nodded.

First, her grandmother cleaned each item. Then, she added hot water and tea powder to her tea bowl. Using a speci**a**l whisk, she stirred them together. Fin**all**y, they each took a sip of tea.

"I learned to make tea from my grandmother," Akira's grandmother said. "She knew exactly how much water to add every time."

She smiled. "Once I told her that she made the best tea in all of Japan," she continued. "I thought she would be pleased. Instead, she shook her head. 'It is not the tea maker or drinker that matters,' she said. 'It is the tea that matters most.'"

Grandmother slowly stood up. "My grandmother was very wise," she said. "But I have often wondered if she was wrong. My per**spect**ive is that everything and everyone in a tea ceremony is important. They all help make it successful."

She went into the kitchen. The warm tea made Akira feel better. But her stomach buzzed with worry. What if Diego was too nervous to ask people to sign the petition?

Akira thought about the tea ceremony. Every part of it was important. If something was missing, the ceremony couldn't happen.

She suddenly understood. She stood up. She ignored the dizzy feeling in her head. She had to find Diego. He couldn't do this without her.

3

Stepping Up

Akira almost reached the elevator when Diego and Baya stepped out of it. Akira asked, "Did you get enough people to sign?"

Diego handed her the clipboard. His mouth stayed in a thin, angry line.

Akira in**spect**ed the petition. Thirty people had signed it. "Is that enough?" she asked.

He shrugged. "I don't know. We'll find out on Saturday." He and Baya began to walk away.

"Wait!" Akira sped up to block his path.

"I shouldn't have said that stuff about you being afraid," she said, out of breath. "But you can't do this without me. I need to tell each person in this building how much the Wishing Tree matters to me. How important the park is to me."

Diego frowned. "It's important to me too, Akira," he said. "And after talking to most of the people in this building today, I can tell you that it matters to a lot of them too."

Akira's throat ached. Had she gotten her grandmother's message wrong? It sounded like Diego **man**aged to do a great job without her. He didn't need her after all.

She blinked away tears. "It had to be hard for you to talk to everyone," she said.

Diego bit his lower lip. "It was hard at first," he said, fin**al**ly. "But it got easier. And Akira, people really do care about the park."

"I'm glad." She smiled. "And I really am sorry. You did great today."

"Thanks. It would have been more fun if you'd been there," he said. "But at least we are ready for the meeting. If you feel better tomorrow, we should figure out a plan for Saturday."

Back in her apartment, Akira lay down on the couch and closed her eyes. She hated being sick when she should have been with Diego today. But maybe it had been good for Diego, she realized. He was braver than either of them thought.

Her grandmother said that every part of the tea ceremony was important. Maybe saving the park was like the tea ceremony. She, Diego, Mr. Crock . . . they all needed to play a part at the meeting on Saturday.

SAVE WISHING TREE
NAME
SAVE WISHING TREE
NAME
Bella
Angela B.
KIKI
PAUL

Suddenly, she sat up. The meeting was Saturday. Her heart sank. Her birthday was Saturday too!

Akira felt like a dark cloud had settled over her. They could get bad news about the park at the meeting. Her birthday would be ruined.

They had only three days to stop that from happening.